Power Up for Fitness

Exercise for Playing Stronger and Running Longer

Charla McMillian and Jonathan Weinress

RED CHAIR PRESS

Let's Move books are produced and published by Red Chair Press.
Red Chair Press LLC PO Box 333 South Egremont, MA 01258
www.redchairpress.com

Note

Look for notes through out this book directed to adults and caregivers. Notes provide background and guidance for each exercise and movement.

Publisher's Cataloging-In-Publication Data

Names: McMillian, Charla. | Weinress, Jonathan.

Title: Power up for fitness : exercise for playing stronger and running longer / by Charla McMillian and Jonathan Weinress.

Description: South Egremont, MA : Red Chair Press, [2018] | Series: Let's move | Includes index, glossary, and suggestions for further reading. | Interest age level: 006-010. | Summary: "Kids know exercise is good for them. But they might not know there are different kinds of exercise ... This book presents easy to follow endurance and muscle strengthening exercises for kids plus informational notes for adults who dare to join in on fitness for a lifetime."--Provided by publisher.

Identifiers: ISBN 9781634404099 (library hardcover) | ISBN 9781634404112 (paperback) | ISBN 9781634404136 (ebook)

Subjects: LCSH: Exercise for children--Juvenile literature. | Physical fitness for children--Juvenile literature. | CYAC: Exercise. | Physical fitness.

Classification: LCC GV443 .M36 2018 (print) | LCC GV443 (ebook) | DDC 613.7/1083/4 [E]--dc23

LCCN: 2017957081

Illustrations: BPI India Pvt. Ltd.

Photographs: iStock.

Printed in the United States of America

0518 1P CGBF18

Table of Contents

TYPES OF EXERCISE

You know exercise is good for you. But you might not know that there are different kinds of exercise. Each helps your body in different ways.

The great news is that a lot of what you like to do probably counts as at least one of these types of exercise. And maybe even more than one. For example, running works your heart and lungs, strengthens your muscles, and makes your bones strong.

Different kinds of exercise are:

1. **Aerobic exercise** to get your heart pumping. Aerobic (air-OH-bik) exercises build endurance. That means you can work and play hard longer without getting so tired.
2. **Stretching exercise**, like toe touches, side-bends, and yoga to help your muscles bend and move easily. Keeping your muscles flexible is important for running and jumping safely.
3. **Muscle strengthening exercise** to make you strong. When someone says they are in good shape it often means their muscles are strong and fit. But having strong muscles helps us sit, stand, run and throw well, too. Let's discover how to "work out" to build muscle and endurance.

Introduction Part 1

by Aziz Jade Derori, M.Ed. Physical Education Teacher

Aerobic exercise builds **endurance**. Endurance, also called "stamina," is an important part of becoming healthy happy and strong. By reading this book, you have taken the first steps to becoming healthy, happy and strong!

Read the whole book before starting. You should try each activity at least three times. Remember, every new activity is difficult at first. Not too long ago, standing, walking and feeding yourself were difficult! Your family may have photos or funny videos of you learning to use a spoon. Did you give up after one or two tries? Of course not! You just kept going and now using a spoon is easy! New activities are always a challenge at first. But just keep going!

After you have tried each activity, you will find there are a few that you really enjoy. Focus on these activities first. Each day you should choose one of the activities to do. Every time you finish an activity your body is getting stronger and healthier! Just keep going!

What is Aerobic Exercise?

Coached by Charla McMillian

Aerobic exercise is a type of activity that makes your heart and lungs stronger. When you do this type of exercise you will breathe faster and your heart will pump harder. But that's okay; it's all good for you. You may even sweat a lot. Many adults use this type of exercise to lose weight and improve their health. For kids, this activity can help you stay focused and get stronger.

Walking

You probably know that walking is good for you. But did you know that walking is an endurance exercise? As an exercise, walking can be very safe. Walking is a great way to see new things and places. You can even walk to compete with others in a race. It's called Race walking!

In Race walking, your goal is to get to the finish as quickly as possible, using the correct form all along the way. Remember that you can never be running when Race walking. Always move forward ***heel–to-toe***, never letting one foot leave the ground like in running. Be sure to pump your arms as you walk because that motion will help you.

Note

Look into Race walking events in your area. Keep in mind that Race walking is a specific type of event, and there are types of techniques that are permitted. Learn what's required, demonstrate it properly, and ensure your child understands the rules and the technique. Find streets near you where you can safely take your children to go walking. Go Race walking on the street as practice. Start with 10–15 minutes total at first. Go Race walking 2–3 days a week at first. After 10–15 minutes, rest awhile before repeating the 10–15-minute exercise.

Jumping Rope

Basic rope jumping uses the standard 2-legged hopping style of jumping rope. Try jumping in place first before adding the rope!

Jump for 3 minutes
Rest for 1 minute
Jump for 3 minutes
Rest for 1 minute
Jump for 3 minutes
Rest

Left-Right Jumping

A

B

Let's make it more difficult! Now each time you jump, land on only one foot, keeping your other foot lifted up with a bent knee. Swing the rope over your head and jump as it passes your feet (picture A). Land on your right foot. On the next rotation, land on your left (picture B). Continue this, as if you were running in place

Jump 1–3 minutes
Rest 1 minute
Jump 1–3 minutes
Rest 1 minute
Jump 1–3 minutes
Rest

Double-unders

You will jump with both legs as in basic jumping, but each time you jump, try to bring the rope around twice before your feet touch the ground.

Double-unders for 1 minute
Rest for 1 minute
Double-unders for 1 minute
Rest for 1 minute
Double-unders for 1 minute
Rest

After using this jump for 1 or 2 weeks, increase your exercise by 30 seconds each. Do that until you can Double-under for 2–3 minutes each time. Remember to rest in between!

Note

You might want to have children practice each jumping exercise for the first week without the jump rope. It might help them feel more confident before adding the rope.

Side-to-side Jumps

Each time you bring the rope around, you will be jumping on both feet like in basic jumping. But now you should jump from one side to the other. Jump to the left, then jump to the right on the 2nd swing.

Jump Side-to-side for 1 minute
Rest for 1 minute
Jump Side-to-side for 1 minute
Rest for 1 minute
Jump Side-to-side for 1 minute
Rest

SAFETY FIRST!

If you feel dizzy or get tired. Just practice the jumps without the rope for awhile!

Jump-rope Jacks

For these, you will do Jumping Jacks without the arm motions. Practice your jumps without tripping on the rope. Make sure you're doing a complete Jumping Jack with feet wide every time the rope comes around.

Jump-rope Jacks for 2 minutes
Rest for 1 minute
Jump-rope Jacks for 2 minutes
Rest for 1 minute
Jump-rope Jacks for 2 minutes
Rest

Note

Kids will naturally want to use their arms when doing jumping jacks. Have the child practice first, jumping wide with arms steady. Then add the rope. If 2 minutes is too difficult, reduce the jumping time of each set to one or one and-a-half minutes each. But try to complete 3 sets.

Scissor-step Jumps

With one foot slightly in front of the other, switch your feet as you jump. Practice this jump a few times without the rope. Then grab your jump rope and be sure you can do the Scissor-step Jump without tripping while swinging the rope overhead.

Scissor-step jump 2 minutes
Rest 1 minute
Scissor-step jump 2 minutes
Rest 1 minute
Scissor-step jump 2 minutes
Rest 1 minute

Note

If your child can't complete a full 2-minute set each time, that's okay. Just reduce the time. Then try to increase the time from one week to the next to build endurance.

Family Fitness First

Never be afraid to get tired, young athlete. The more you can convince yourself to keep exercising, to complete the race or competition, the better you will perform, and the more you will inspire other kids younger than you. Have a great time, and keep moving!

Note

Mom or Dad: Do you like to walk fast? An activity that many adults do is called race walking. Race walking has a very specific technique and several important rules. According to most experts, you will do better studying and learning the technique slowly before you use it in any competition and before you try to do it regularly for training. [Check this out from USA Track and Field: www.usatf.org/Sports/Race-Walking.aspx]

Race walking is done by many different athletes for many different reasons and with many different results. Runners who have gotten injured often try to find another sport that causes less injury. People who walk for fitness often look for ways to get into shape even faster. And people who have not exercised before often find Race walking a safe way to get into exercise. Race walking requires a great deal of focus and concentration on the technique while you're doing it. Many adult athletes do not have this amount of focus and will not concentrate. As a result, they give up on the sport. See if you have what it takes.

Build your skills first when you start race walking. As you get better with your technique, you will get faster and faster. Be honest with yourself. Mastering the technique might take you as little as two months or it might take you up to two years. Work hard, be patient and be diligent.

Introduction Part 2

Before we begin, you will need to gather a few items from home. Ask an adult to help you find an easy-to-move chair with a back (like a folding chair). And you will need weights such as two cans of soup from your kitchen cabinet, or two 2-pound hand weights. You will use these 'weights' to push and pull your muscles.

Now that you have your equipment together, let's discuss how you will be working out. When you pick up your weights and move your arms and legs in a certain way that is called a **repetition**. To perform a repetition (or rep) a certain number of times is called a **set**. So if you do an exercise once, that would be one repetition; and if you do that exercise eight times without stopping, you will have completed eight repetitions! That would be one set of 8 reps. Got it?

Exercise is good for all of us. But, it should be fun even when it is a challenge! You should have fun exploring fitness and exercise for a lifetime of good health.

What does "working out" mean?

Coached by Jonathan Weinress

Have you ever wanted to be able to run faster? Or jump higher? Or throw a ball really far? You can learn to do this and more by strength training or "working out." That means you are working your muscles to get stronger.

When you run or play, you use your muscles to push and pull yourself along. Sometimes after all this running and playing you get really tired. In this book you'll find exercises to help your muscles learn to work harder, so you can have more fun.

Note

Your child is still growing and his/her muscles and tendons are already stressed just trying to grow. So don't expect big changes in your child's muscles at first. This introduction to exercise is all about building a lifetime habit of fitness. It's up to you to make it fun for the whole family!

Bicep Curls

Pick up your weights. Sit in your chair. Sit up tall with your tummy tight. Bring your arms to your sides with palms facing forward. On a count of 1, 2, 3 bring your hands up to your shoulders. Be sure your elbows do not move forward! At the top of the movement squeeze your arm muscles. Feel it? That's your bicep working!

Now lower your hands back down to your sides. Raising and lowering your forearm like this is called a Curl. You curl your arm up and uncurl back down to your sides for each rep. Remember to count 1, 2, 3 on the way down too. Try to do your Curls six or seven times.

Note

Your child can vary this exercise by simply standing up or alternating arms. Start in a chair, as standing to curl requires balance. Don't use heavier cans or weights until your child can do these comfortably.

Tackle the Triceps

The muscle in the back of your arm behind the bicep is called the tricep. The bicep and tricep are partners that work together to help us move, reach, and pull. Think about this. When you get a glass of water, it is your bicep that helps you bring the glass to your mouth. And when you take the glass away from your mouth to put it down, you use your triceps muscle.

Note

When you or your child feels as though you could keep going before fatigue sets in, you might add another 2–6 repetitions. Be sure to rest 30 to 60 seconds between reps to allow muscles to recover. Adding one or two reps every 10 to 14 days is usually a safe rule of thumb; and exercising 3 days a week is just about right.

Vary your workout by mixing up the order in which you and your child perform the exercises. Our examples use counts of 3 seconds for each direction up or down. You may want to try lowering weights in counts of 2 while raising weights in counts of 5 seconds. Try to change something in your routines every few weeks to keep your muscles firing!

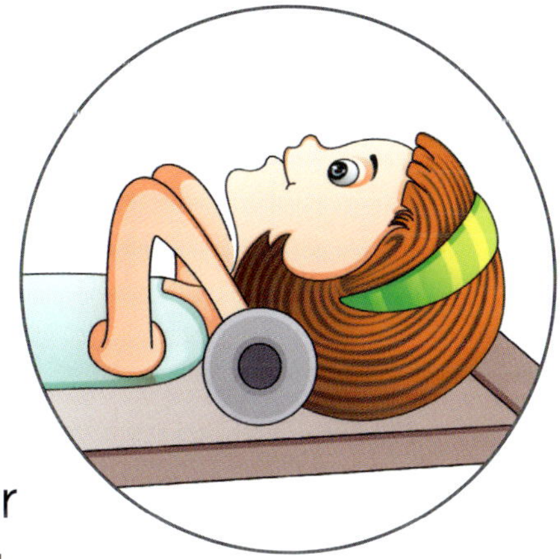

To work the back of your arms, begin by lying flat on the floor with your knees bent. Choose weights for each hand. Bring your arms straight up. On a count of 1, 2, 3 fold your arms and lower your hands down to the side of your head by your ears. Keep your elbows straight up. Then unfold your arms back up to the ceiling, counting 1, 2, 3 on the way up. Try this six times at first. Move slowly—**Remember Slow is Safe!**

Note

Try to make sure the child's shoulders stay on the floor while the arms are raised to the ceiling.

Chest Press

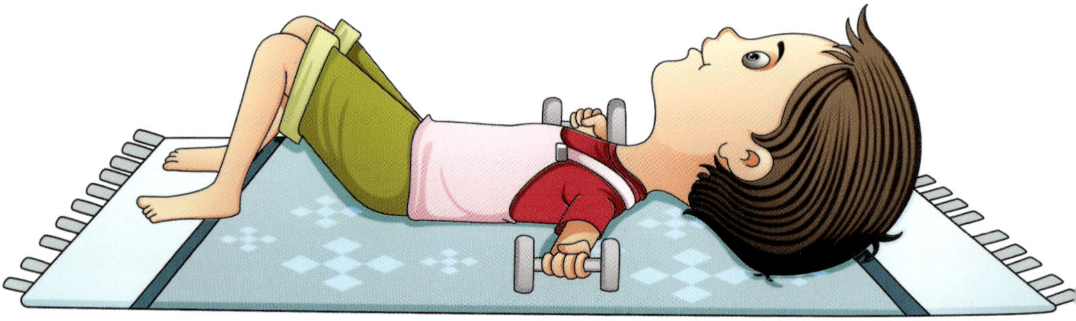

Your chest muscles are called **pectoral** muscles. You use the pectorals all the time. They are important if you want to push up from the ground. When you hang or swing from monkey bars you use your pectoral muscles.

Lie down on the floor with your knees bent. With the weights in your hands move your arms out away from your body until your elbows are even with your shoulders—or as straight as you can move them. (The backs of your arms, triceps, are on the ground.) Now bend your arms and bring them up with palms facing away. The backs of your arms should be on the ground and elbows bent. You should be making a letter 'L' with each arm.

Note

Remember to monitor the breath. During strength training it is best to breathe out, or exhale, on the exertion then take a deep breath in before the next rep begins.

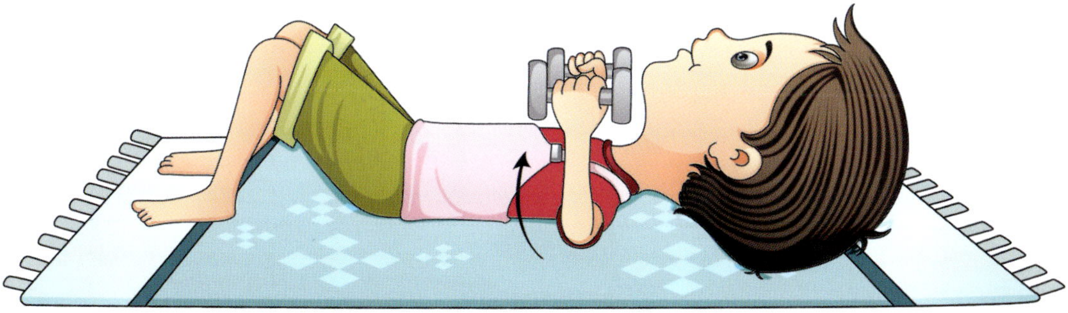

Take a deep breath in and as you blow out your breath slowly count 1, 2, 3 and straighten your arms overhead. Now, breathe in and slowly bring the backs of your arms to the floor again. Try it again—slowly—for 4 to 6 times if you can.

Push-Ups

A push-up is a pressing motion for your upper body. Get down on the floor on your knees and hands. Hands should be palm down on the floor and keep your arms straight. Think about looking like a table.

Note

When your child is ready for a challenge, have them try a push up with legs out fully straight behind them. Keep the back straight and push up to straight arms. This is much harder, so try only a few at first.

Now bend your elbows and lean into your arms, chest, and shoulders. Slowly bend your elbows until your arms are just even with your shoulders. Then, push your hands into the floor and straighten your arms back to the starting position. Did you keep your back straight and your tummy tight? Keep at it until you can do 10 to 12 strong reps!

Crunches

If you lie down on the floor and try to sit up with just your upper body, you are doing a sit-up! Your stomach muscles are strong and they do many things such as helping you sit in a chair, throw a ball and even lie in bed reading a book. So it is important we keep our **abdominals** or stomach muscles strong.

Note

An adult can help by making sure the head stays back in alignment with the spine. Imagine an apple tucked under the child's chin. Do not let the child round, or pull with their arms. Remember Slow is Safe. It should take 2–3 seconds to come up and 2–3 seconds to lower back down. For a variation, try putting the child's feet up on a chair seat, with knees bent instead of flat on the floor.

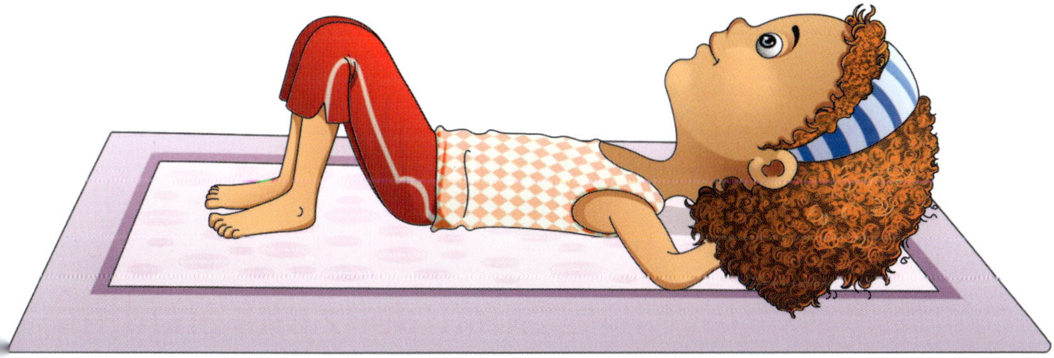

Lie down on the floor with knees bent and feet flat. Place your fingertips by your ears with elbows out from your sides. Ready? Now tighten your stomach muscles, squeeze them hard and slowly lift your head and shoulders off the ground. Don't worry if you don't get far, just a few inches should do it! Breathe out (exhale) and slowly lower yourself back down flat to the floor. Try for a set of 10 reps.

Back Rows

Have you ever been told to *Stand tall* or *Stand up straight*? We use our back muscles for standing well. Strong back muscles also help when you play volleyball, softball on even when you throw a flying disc!

To build a strong back, get one of your weight cans and a chair. Hold the weight in one hand and reach forward to put your other hand palm-down on the seat of the chair. Keep the arm straight. Next, step back with one leg (same side as the hand holding the weight). Your front leg should be bent slightly at the knee. Keep both feet on the floor with your chest up and hips facing the chair.

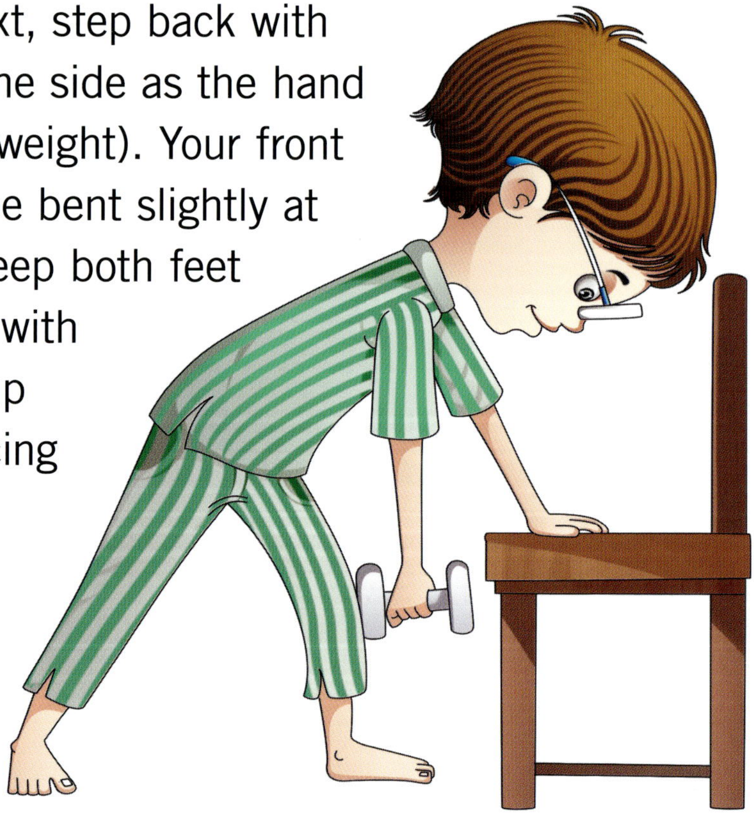

Ready? Reach forward with the weight until your arm is fully extended in front of you. Now pull your arm back slowly while your elbow pulls up (like a wing) and your hand with the weight comes back to the side of your chest. Try a few times until you are ready for a set of 10 to 12 reps. Give yourself time. Your muscles are stretching and working hard!

WORDS TO KNOW

abdominals: the muscles across the stomach, below the ribs.

endurance: the ability to do something difficult or hard

form: the correct way to place and hold the body during an exercise. Using the correct form helps prevent injury.

pectorals: the chest muscles.

repetition: the complete full movement of an exercise; often called one rep.

set: a certain number of movements or reps to complete an exercise.

tempo: the time it takes to complete a repetition. You may change the tempo to make an exercise easier or more difficult.

READ MORE

Galloway, Jeff. *Fit Kids, Smarter Kids*. Oxford Press, 2007.

Herrington, Lisa M. *I Like to Exercise*. Children's Press, 2015.

Labrecque, Ellen. *Stamina: Get Stronger and Play Longer!* Heinemann-Raintree, 2013.

Marisco, Katie. *Exercise!* (21st Century Junior Library) Cherry Lake Publishing, 2015.

Rockwell, Lizzy. *The Busy Body Book: A Kids' Guide to Fitness*. Dragonfly Books, 2008.

INDEX

About the Authors

Charla McMillian is a former Marine Corps Officer and the creator of FitBoot™ Basic Training for Professionals, New England's original boot camp fitness training program. She is the author of *Boot Camp Abs: Get Rock-Hard Abs with Former Marine Captain Charla McMillian* (Fair Winds Press). Charla is certified by the National Strength and Conditioning Association as a Certified Strength and Conditioning Specialist®.

Jonathan Weinress is a certified trainer and therapist who enjoys working out for a lifetime of fitness with his young grandson Malachi. Jonathan lives and works in Great Barrington, Massachusetts.